SIMON AND SCHUSTER

SIMON AND SCHUSTER
First published in Great Britain in 2012 by Simon and Schuster UK Ltd
1st Floor, 222 Gray's Inn Road, London WC1X 8HB
A CBS Company

Based on the television series Mike the Knight
© 2012 HIT (MTK) Limited/Nelvana Limited. A United Kingdom-Canada Co-production.

ISBN 978-0-85707-588-8
Printed and bound in China
10 9 8 7 6 5 4 3 2
www.simonandschuster.co.uk

Mike the Knight

and the Fluttering Favour

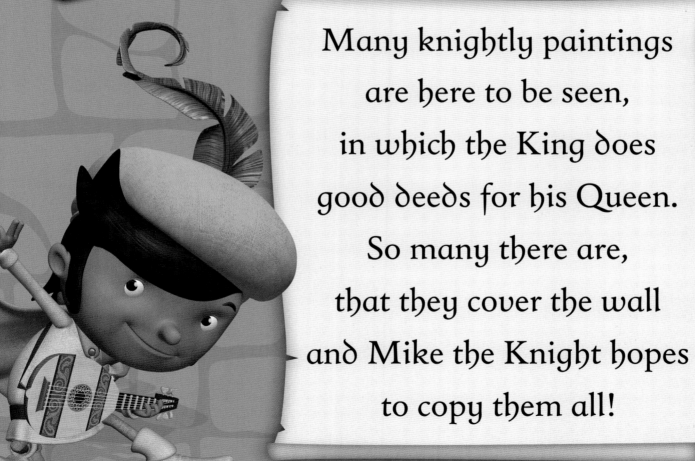

Many knightly paintings
are here to be seen,
in which the King does
good deeds for his Queen.
So many there are,
that they cover the wall
and Mike the Knight hopes
to copy them all!

Great knights are sometimes rewarded for their good deeds.

Mike was looking at a fine tapestry of his dad, the King, clutching a lance decorated with scarves.

"Those are called favours," smiled Queen Martha. "I gave them to your father when he did knightly deeds for his Kingdom."

Mike was admiring another favour on a lance, when Evie marched in.

"That scarf will be perfect for my spell," Evie squealed.

"That's a knightly favour," said Mike. "You can't just take it. You have to win it by doing a good deed, like helping someone out."

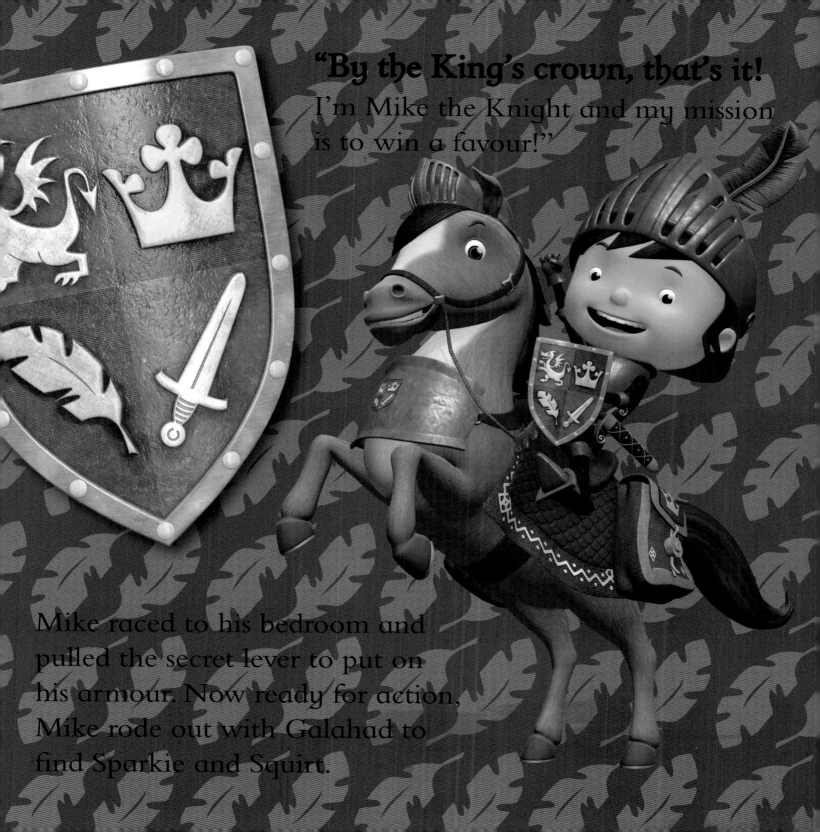

"By the King's crown, that's it!
I'm Mike the Knight and my mission
is to win a favour!"

Mike raced to his bedroom and
pulled the secret lever to put on
his armour. Now ready for action,
Mike rode out with Galahad to
find Sparkie and Squirt.

When Mike drew his enchanted sword, a mop appeared. "I wonder how I can use this?"

There was no time to think it over. The knight-in-training needed to help someone, fast!

In the village, Mike spotted Mr Blacksmith.
"Good morning, sir! Can I help you?"

Mr Blacksmith was being lifted in the air by a
shimmer of stars. He looked a little worried, but
he said, "Young Evie's helping me with my bag."

"It's knights who win favours!" Mike said to Evie.

"This is my good deed!" Evie spun round and the magic floating spell was instantly broken.

Mr Blacksmith tumbled out of the sky, and landed in a hay cart with a **T-H-U-D!**

Mike and the dragons rushed ahead to find another good deed to do.

"The blacksmith has been bending these straight poles into horseshoes," said Mike. "We can do that to help him!"

Mike picked out a metal pole. Sparkie breathed fire to heat it and then shaped it into a horseshoe. Squirt sprayed the horseshoe with water to cool it down.

"Hey!" cried an angry voice. "I was going to do that."
Evie pointed her wand at Mr Blacksmith's poles.

"*With this magic*
I can't lose,
Turn these long poles
Into shoes!"

CRASH! BANG! CLATTER!

A noisy bunch of metal shoes, boots and slippers dropped out of the sky!

By the time Mr Blacksmith got back to the workshop, there wasn't a straight pole left in his wheelbarrow.

"I was making old horseshoes straight," Mr Blacksmith groaned. "Now I'll have to start all over again."

"By the dragon's tooth, that's it!" said Mike. "Our good
deed can be to make the blacksmith's workshop fresh
and clean."
Evie beat Mike to it with her spell:

*"I'll make this workshop
Really clean,
With the biggest hose
You've ever seen!"*

The magic worked!
A huge, green hose
appeared. Evie
started to wash
down the walls.

When his sister
wasn't looking, the
young knight put
his foot on the hose.

The water stopped
at once.

"Where's the water
gone?" wondered
Evie.

Mike picked up the hose. "Galahad! Let it flow!"
"But it's my hose and my good deed," shouted Evie.
"I'm telling Mum!"
Mike dashed after Evie, leaving the dragons to deal with
the splashy hose.

The hose flicked left and right. Squirt tried to grab the end, but Evie's spell was too strong.

"Hang on, Squirt!" cried Sparkie.

"What's the problem here?"

The hose sprayed Mr Blacksmith with chilly water, knocking him down.

At the castle, Mike and Evie were fighting in the throne room.

"Ha!" cried Evie, pulling the scarf off its lance. "I won the favour!"

Mike snatched it back. "No! I won it!"

RRRrrrrippppp! The precious favour tore in half.

Queen Martha hurried into the chamber.

"I was in the village when a huge hose-monster appeared, spitting water everywhere!" she gasped. "And what has happened to your father's favour?"

"It's my fault," said Evie in a little voice. "I made the hose-monster with magic."

"But I left the hose running," added Mike. "It's my fault, too."

Instead of working together, Mike and Evie had worked against each other. Now they agreed they wanted to put things right!

"Can you make it stop, Evie?" asked Mike.

"With a wave of my wand
That hose must go,
Stop its water's
Thrashing flow!"

The hose disappeared but Mr Blacksmith and his workshop were still covered in icky, sticky mud!

"We're really sorry," said Mike, pulling out his mop sword. **"It's time to be a knight and do it right!"**

Evie grabbed a bucket. "We're a team now!"

Mike and Evie got to work. While they scrubbed away the mud, Sparkie and Squirt straightened out all the old horseshoes.

"My workshop's never been so clean!" chuckled Mr Blacksmith. "I'm very proud of you two."

"And so am I," beamed Queen Martha.

"I've got something for you both," said the Queen, holding up a pair of matching scarves.

Each half of the King's torn favour had been stitched into a beautiful new one. Mike felt very proud. It was a shared favour for a shared good deed!

HUZZAH!